For Michael
on his sixth birthday

With love from Grams

THE MAGIC REED
OF
THE WOODPECKER

THE MAGIC REED
OF
THE WOODPECKER

by
Thomas W. Longazel

DORRANCE & COMPANY, INCORPORATED
828 LANCASTER AVENUE • BRYN MAWR, PENNSYLVANIA 19010
Publishers Since 1920

To Dad, for countless hours spent
telling his endless stories.

The Magic Reed of the Woodpecker

Since the beginning of time man has dreamed of finding some magic or secret to unlock doors. I believe if he ever gained this gift, he would use it to do good deeds and help others, rather than harm them.

This tale, about a man who found such magic, is one that was told to me and others by my father. Like most of the old-timers, my dad was a great storyteller and could make you gasp for breath, make you feel sad, or make you feel happy. This gift they had was an art you could not buy at any price.

The story was told one evening when I was about nine and all the old-timers sat around talking about finding a new place in life. It was the first time I had heard it and my mind has been wondering ever since. I know it made me hope that I might find the magic someday. And maybe after you hear it, you too might look for the secret.

From the first day I heard the tale I called it, "The Magic Reed of the Woodpecker."

The story can best be understood, perhaps, by a person who has lived with deep superstitions. I grew up around coal mining towns where most people believed in legends and superstitions. Life was hard around the mines, although it was tough anywhere in those days. The people were good, hard working, and most of all, trusting. Miners were always looking for hope, and superstition played an important part of their lives.

I would like to tell you the tale the way I heard it, but first I want to give you some idea of the events that led up to this kind of tale. They were events not unusual to mining towns, but for those readers who did not grow up in that life, they may help explain the need for legends and myths—the need for something to keep alive the fires of hope.

When some event took place around the mines that caused hardship and danger, like an explosion, a cave-in, or a rock slide, most of the men would sit around and hope. This is when they would gather around in the evenings and tell stories or listen to them, trying to get up enough nerve to go back into that black hole called the mines.

As a kid around the mines you had to learn the signs that made up this kind of life. Sounds were very important, and one of the most important was the mine whistle. You had to know what was taking place when it blew. At 5:00 A.M. when it blew, that was to wake the town and the miners for the day's work. At 7:00 A.M. it would blow to start the trip into the mines. This was when all the miners would get into the mine cars, about fifty of them coupled together, to be lowered into the mine by a heavy cable and hoist. At noon it blew, and again at 4:00 P.M., when the men would ride the cars and be pulled from the mines by the same cable and hoist that lowered them in. At 7:00 P.M. was one of the most important soundings of the whistle, for it meant that the mines would be working the next day.

When the whistle blew during working hours, and continued to blow, you knew that it meant trouble at the mines, and everyone would make their way to the mine yard to see how bad it was and who was injured. Most of the people lived with this worry day in and day out. I know I did even as a kid. I rushed to the main yard several times in my life because I had my father and brother working there.

One day early in May, the whistle never even had a chance to blow.

There were a few hundred men going to work in Mine #3 early this Monday morning. They had just entered a short time before, and many were still on their way to the face where they worked, when the gas exploded inside the mine.

The force of the explosion ripped the sides out of the fan house and put the fan out of commission. It was several hours later that the fan was repaired enough to blow fresh air into the gas-filled mine.

The women had just sent their men off to work, like any other morning, and were busy cleaning up the kitchen. The doors and windows were closed, but still all of them heard it—the chilling sound "WHOOMP" that all dreaded to hear. As they caught their breath and stopped dead in their tracks, the earth trembled beneath their feet and their houses shook.

Mothers, wives, sisters, and brothers grabbed wraps and began running to the mine, many of them clutching babies or holding onto small children. One glance at the shattered fan house and the dust and smoke now coming out of the mine drift told them their worst fears had been realized.

You could hear the screams and shrieks above all other noise and you could see the heart-torn grief of the women. They tried to push in close to the area like a big wave, and some of the men tried to talk to them and finally had to restrain them.

At that moment, I think, all petty dislikes and hard feelings were gone. You could see how each one tried to comfort the other.

In the minutes that followed, others arrived: the doctor, almost always first on hand when the men needed help, the priest, the ministers, and the undertaker. The doctor set up a medical station and a temporary morgue was set up in one of the mine buildings. Things began to move and more men arrived to help in the rescue.

The rescuers worked in relays all morning, wearing gas masks because the afterdamp of carbon monoxide that followed the explosion was starting to build up in the sections. Several bodies were found within hours after the blast, then a

3

few others, and then about ten along the main heading. They made the decision to leave the dead inside until survivors could be taken out. Some of the men who had been near the slope were virtually uninjured and walked out of the mine.

They were lucky.

The fears grew as the day wore on, fears that another explosion might take place. Men, women, and children stood by, waiting for the bodies to be taken from the mine. When the first miners, living and dead, were brought outside, the women stood on tiptoes, stretching their necks to see, straining their ears to hear a name. Some miners were loaded on trucks and taken to the hospital where the doctor would examine each of the dead to make sure no life remained. Then the bodies were hauled to the makeshift morgue.

At times a name would sweep the crowd, then a few more. You could hear the sighs of relief from some and shrieks of agony from others. A mother or widow would turn away in grief, or just fall to the ground and have to be carried away.

It was a practice in the mines that when small accumulations of gas were found, they were burned off with flames from the carbide lamps that men used for light in the mines. My dad told me how they used to do this. He said that a flame would result that could shoot out several hundred feet. No one knew whether this explosion was caused by such a burn-off or by an accidental ignition. It probably was set off by some miner with an open flame on his carbide lamp going through a pocket of gas; but this will never be determined.

The force of the blast was considerable. Metal doors were blown away and thick brick walls were leveled. Locomotives, mine motors used to pull the coal cars, were lifted off the tracks. Mud in heavy layers was blown on the walls and onto the sides of the mine cars.

The search for living and dead continued through the day and night and into the next day. With the passing hours, hopes faded for finding any additional survivors. The crowd of hundreds waited outside for any word from below. And the crowd shrank each time bodies were removed from the mine and mourners were led away.

The next day, and the next, men stood on the street and watched the passing of trucks coming from the mines and heading toward the morgue. Each time they would only shake their heads and say a prayer. Earlier the men stayed close to the hall used as a morgue, but the sight of friends' charred bodies made them move their vigil.

Funerals had to be held, in groups and singly. When several miners belonged to the same church, a joint service was held.

Work went very slowly cleaning out the mine, and for the miners the thought of going back still hurt. Most had always lived with this fear, but now it was stronger.

Some of the miners talked about that day and remembered how they groped and stumbled through dark passages, gasping in the bad air and crawling on their hands and knees through the water and mud, fighting for their next breath; how they had fallen and some could not get up again; and how the ones who did get up fought the deadly fumes, the darkness, the fears, knowing that death stalked all around them and that they might be the next. Some had wandered about for hours, finding enough air to breathe and survive long enough to get to the outside. Some formed in groups, lying on the floor face down to suck in any air that had not been stained with afterdamp. They said many men died in the explosion and fire, but far more perished from the afterdamp that followed. Some of the men said they tried to joke and curse, but most cried and prayed. It was hard to find any humor when they knew life was nearly at its end. Instead they say they prayed and asked for God's mercy.

Days passed and the rescuers worked hard and long to find miners still trapped in parts of the mine, but with the timbers ripped out and gas still in the mines, it was difficult going.

They brought in canaries to test the air for gas, and if the bird died they had to find some way to remove the gas in the area. My father used to tell us about rats in the mines and how they would leave when a rock fall was going to take place. They always made their way out of these danger areas beforehand, and the miners came to respect this sign and follow along.

Several days passed and all was cleared out of the mines. Now it was being readied for a new work day. Everyone that worked in the mines knew that the day would come for them to return. What else was left for them to do?

And when the whistle sent out the call for them to return to work, the survivors saw a lot of new faces replacing old friends lost to this mine.

I guess it must be a gift from God, because it didn't take long for them to get back into the swing of things and for the town to get back to its old way of life. Of course everyone knew that it might happen again, but this time they would try to prevent it. The mine owners promised to make more inspections and set up teams and even said they would have a first aid post in the mines. But would this really be any help?

In the days right after the accident the men didn't take much time out for storytelling. I guess because they had to gather up enough strength for each day's work.

But it was only a few months after the explosion, late in July, that another day of sadness was to take place. The whistle sounded and it seemed like it would never stop blowing.

At the mine site it was told that there was a rock fall and two men were crushed to death. They said one man lived until they removed him from the mines; the other was dead at the spot.

All the miners came home early from work this day because of the accident, and supper was ready a little early. This meant the men would be outside on the porch sooner, or on the street, to talk about the rock fall.

Metro, the man who lived next door to us in the double

house, made the porch first and my dad followed. Pete, who lived in the next house, came over and started to tell my father and Metro about the rock fall and how he helped to get the men out. It was only a few minutes later that more men came and sat on the steps near the top of the porch.

I guess they just wanted to talk and get it off their minds. First they told each other what they knew of the day's events and how shaken they were over men being hurt and killed. Then they sat for awhile, and when the pipes and cigars were lit, smoking seemed to relax them and the stories started.

One of the men said, "Mike, how about the woodpecker story? I never did hear how it ended."

Mike, my father, replied, "I really don't know if it had an end, or if you could find one." But then Dad took a puff on his cigar and said, "OK," and started off with the tale, while I got settled in to make sure I didn't miss any part of it.

As the story goes, men have always wanted to find the secret that would unlock every door, and in the coal fields they tell of how the woodpecker has this special magic.

What you must do first is find a woodpecker's nest that has young birds in it, and wait until the mother leaves its nest in search of food for the babies.

You then have to climb up to the hole and drive in a wooden peg to block the hole to the nest. Then you must hide in the woods, or under cover nearby, so that the mother bird cannot see or hear you, and wait.

When the bird returns to find her nest blocked, the cries of her young ones inside will make her very upset. She will try everything to remove the peg, clawing at the peg and trying to peck it out with her beak. But if all her attempts fail she will leave and search for a "magic reed."

After awhile the mother bird returns with a blade of grass in her beak. As you watch her from under cover you will see her touch it to the peg, at the same time trying to stay to one side of the hole, and when you see what happens to the peg you will know why.

If nothing happens at the touch of the grass, she becomes even more upset and leaves to return with another blade of grass. Some have told of watching her make the try three times before anything happened.

While you sit watching this ritual it is hard to imagine that anything is going to happen. But just about the time you are growing tired of waiting, she touches the reed to the peg and you hear a loud crack.

The plug shoots out of the hole, flying like a bullet into the brush. Then the mother goes into the nest, and after a brief check inside, she comes out with the reed in her beak and flies off again, only to return without the reed. Where did she take it? This is one thing that no one had been able to find out.

It was a mystery what kind of power this reed had to remove the peg with such force, and this strange power was something men wanted to gain and have for their own. The few who had seen a woodpecker use a magic reed had tried to follow her, but to follow a bird in flight in the woods is impossible. The tale goes on to tell of a group of men that formed three circles around the nest, and even then they could not follow her flight. The woodpecker had the secret and kept it to herself.

Had kept it, that is, until a man named Michael Juddac happened to be in the right place at the right time.

Juddac, as he was called by most folks around, made part of his income working as a herdsman during the summer and did woodworking jobs in the fall and winter. Many of the people around mining towns kept a cow to help provide milk and cheese for their family. This helped to feed a large family and made the going a little easier. Juddac would watch the cows for people at a charge of two dollars a month and he would mix up feed for the cows, his own blend, and people came from miles around to buy his feed. He cared for the animals as if they were his own, and the people knew this and trusted him.

Juddac was well liked by everyone and they told him so. Several farmers that lived nearby would come to him for help when their cattle were sick and would have him mix up feed to help get them well. They wanted Juddac to start his own feed mill because he had the best grade of mix around.

When people hired him to make or repair furniture, they never asked him what the cost would be; they all knew that the work would be good and the cost would be fair.

The right place. Well, Juddac stopped one day while he was taking care of the cows to have some lunch, and he built a fire to heat up his coffee and roast his bacon. He left the area for a few minutes to gather some wood for the fire and when he returned, he saw a strange thing taking place. Over the fire was a bird fluttering—a woodpecker. It didn't see him, and he stayed back in the brush and kept very still to see what was going on.

It was a red-headed woodpecker and in its beak was a piece of grass. It fluttered over the fire seeming to look for the right spot, then dropped the blade of grass into the fire and flew away. Juddac, knowing of the woodpecker tale and how everyone had tried to find out what she did with the reed, felt he had the answer at last.

He sat down in a daze, his mind still seeing the bird destroy the blade of grass. Then Juddac made up his mind not to tell anyone what he had witnessed today, but to find a way to recover this magic reed.

That evening when he returned home with the cows, he sat down for a long time in the barn where he kept his own cow and tried to make some plans as to how he could recover the reed. He decided that first he must find a woodpecker's nest and then go on with the same routine used by the others, with a few new ideas of his own.

The follwing day while he was taking care of the cows in

the fields, he went into the wooded area and looked up in every tree in search of a woodpecker or its nest. This went on for a few days, and he had never before realized how hard it was to find a woodpecker, let alone one with a nest and young birds in it. Each time he tried to rest, his mind kept him busy thinking of how he could get this reed. When he went into the woods in search of a nest, he could only think of what he might do with the magic if he recovered it and wonder if it really was filled with all the power the tales made it out to have.

A few more days passed before his search paid off. Just at the edge of a wooded area stood an old dried-out tree, and looking up, Juddac saw a woodpecker go into a hole in the tree. The bird had some food in its beak so he knew that it must have young birds in the nest and had just returned to feed them. He went a little closer and could hear the babies inside making a fuss. Now he was sure that this was the setting.

Juddac waited several minutes, that seemed like hours to him, for the mother to leave her nest again in search of food. Finally, out she came.

He hurried over to the tree and made the climb up to the hole, about fifteen feet high. When he looked inside he saw four small birds, mouths wide open, just as wide as his, he thought. He took a few measurements of the hole and then made his way back down the tree. This had to be done fast because the mother could return to tend her babies at any time. Going back to the edge of the woods, Juddac sat down to watch the cows graze in the field and at the same time he studied all the land marks to make sure of the location. For tomorrow was to be the day.

That evening, when his cow was taken care of and his meal finished, Juddac went to his small woodshop and started to make the wood plug to be used in recovering the reed. The plug made and a few other items prepared, he went back into his house.

10

His plans for the next morning's venture called for a small fire near the edge of the woods, so he could stay hidden until the woodpecker dropped the reed, then rush out and recover it from the fire. He also had to find a way of keeping the fire from getting too hot, so he came up with the idea of placing some green wood on top to keep it cool and hold down the flames. This would be a good way, he thought.

One more important plan was that he had to stay to one side of the field, because on the other side was a small house where an old couple made their home and Juddac wanted to make sure they couldn't see what he was doing.

When all of these plans were complete, he went to bed, but sleep didn't come easy. He tossed and turned most of the night. At 5:00 A.M. he got out of bed and started to get ready for the day's work, eager to get to the nest. I guess the only thing he had on his mind was the joy of thinking how he would recover the reed.

After stopping to pick up the neighbors' cows he turned the cows toward the field. That day it seem like it took forever, and even the cows were moving more slowly, so he thought. All Juddac could think of was reaching the field and then going to the old tree with the nest to wait for the woodpecker to make her move. He could see himself up in the tree recovering the reed, but he wasn't there yet.

Now the cows were on their own and Juddac made his way to the tree. He went to the site and gathered some wood for the fire he would build and made a few other plans, checking his pocket for the peg and making sure he had his matches. When this was done he found a spot at the edge of the clearing and prepared the wood. He knew that everything had to be timed just right. He would light the fire when the bird left the nest, then climb up the tree and drive in the peg. This done, he must hurry back to his hiding place and wait for the life-long dream of many men to come true to Juddac himself.

Everything was ready now, so Juddac sat back under cover and waited for the moment to come. Just a few minutes passed and as he glanced up, out came the woodpecker and flew off across the field. Now was the time. He hurried to the tree, made the climb, and drove in the peg. As he started to return to his hiding place he thought, Darn, I forgot to light the fire! Running back to the pile of wood he lit a match and started the fire, blowing on it to make a faster start. He was out of breath when he finally returned to his hiding place. He now had to rest up and get ready for the bird to make her return.

The woodpecker came flying back to the nest, and when she found it blocked, made such a fuss that Juddac felt guilty for what he had done. Wings flapping, and now pecking at the peg, she tried everything to remove the plug, but with no success. She flew away and Juddac thought surely she was going for the magic reed. The bird returned again and this time she tried to pull out the peg with her claws, but this too failed, and off she flew toward the field.

Juddac sat there and wondered if he was wasting his time, or just putting this poor bird through pain for no reason. But about five minutes later the woodpecker returned to the nest, and lo and behold, in her bill was a blade of grass.

As Juddac waited and watched from his spot in the woods, she positioned herself to one side of the plug and paused to make sure that everything was just right. Then she touched the reed to the peg, and at that moment he heard a loud crack, and the peg went hurtling through the air and into the field.

The woodpecker looked into her nest, and now sure her babies were safe and free, she made her flight in the direction of the fire at the edge of the woods, but when she got near the fire she made a turn and flew toward the small house across the field. The house where the old folks lived had a fireplace they used for cooking and heating the house. The woodpecker landed on top of the chimney and moved to the center and dropped the blade of grass into the opening.

Juddac, seeing what happened, felt sick. He couldn't move

and didn't feel he wanted to. What went wrong? How close I came, he thought, to recovering the reed and yet how far away. His mind started to race like a freight train as he stood near the edge of the woods and watched the mother make her return to the nest and her family.

What? What went wrong? Juddac asked himself. For the rest of the day the cows took care of themselves, because Juddac was in no mood to think of them or worry about them. The only thing he had on his mind was the magic reed. It seemed the more he tried to forget about what happened, the more it bothered him.

He had seen it and knew that the woodpecker had the secret and knew what the woodpecker did with the magic reed. He wanted to tell someone about his near success today, but he knew he would have to keep it to himself.

After a day of just sitting around, it was finally time to start home with the cows. Juddac stopped once again to look at the tree, then turned the cows homeward.

He dropped off the cows, finished his work around the barn, and washed up to start his evening meal. While he was eating supper and still deep in thought about the reed, an idea came to him.

Juddac jumped up from the table and went to an old chest that sat in a corner of his bedroom. Raising the lid, he started to look for what he now felt would help him recover the reed. From the chest he took out a bright red piece of cloth, so red that in the light it appeared the color of fire. In his mind he was already making plans for the next day's try. That night, as before, Juddac, tried to sleep but could only think of the next morning when he could go back to the nest. It didn't come easy but sleep did come at last, after a thousand new ideas had flashed in his mind as how to get the magic reed.

If I didn't have to be so careful not to arouse suspicion, he thought, I could go to the spot near the nest and spend the night. Of course going there without the cows would make it known that something was taking place, because up to now no one had any idea of his find. Better leave well enough alone, Juddac said to himself, and finally fell asleep.

Morning came and he up and had his coffee and a bite to eat and was ready to put his new idea to work. He went along with his same routine of gathering up the cows and heading for the field, with only one change, going off in a different direction just to make sure no one would follow him.

It took him about an hour to arrive at the site of his failure the day before, but once the cows were in the field he moved very fast. On his way to the field he had gathered the wood for the fire and also four wooden stakes, about two feet long, that would play an important part in the recovery of the magic reed.

He made the same moves as he did the day before, but this time he added the four stakes sticking up around the firewood. He placed some stones around the firewood, too, to insure a better fire, hoping it would make the smoke rise and flow straight up from the fire. When he completed this, once again Juddac made his way to the edge of the woods to take cover so he would not be noticed by the woodpecker.

He reached into his pocket to make sure the cloth was there and the tin box that held his matches.

The time seemed to drag out even longer than the day before, because he was sure that today was the day. As he waited, his thoughts were on what he might do with this magic reed. He thought about the good he could do and the money he could make showing off his new-found power. He was even tempted by the thought of using it to unlock doors and vaults where money was stored, and becoming very rich. But, No, he said to himself, you shouldn't use a power like that to steal.

About the time Juddac was deepest in thought, out popped the woodpecker and flew to the ground below the nest, then returned to the nest. She came out once more and flew off across the field. He wasn't sure how long she would be gone on her first flight so he just waited to make sure. The bird was gone only a few minutes and then returned to the nest and fed her young ones. After the feeding she came out and flew off again, this time flying higher than before. Juddac knew it was time to make his move.

He rushed out of the woods, making sure to light the fire, and ran to the tree. With the peg in his hand he made the climb up the tree and once again drove the plug into the hole. When he hurried back to the fire Juddac put on a few green sticks of wood to keep it from burning too hot. He then took from his pocket the bright red cloth, which now looked even brighter in the morning sunlight, and placed it on top of the four stakes he had pushed into the ground around the fire. Making sure that the cloth was secured to the stakes, he left for his hiding place at the edge of the woods and sat down to wait.

He was none too soon, because about the time he got settled in, the woodpecker returned to the tree. Once again she found her nest blocked and her babies inside making a fuss. This seemed to upset her even more today because she became still more frantic than the day before. The bird dropped the food she was holding in her beak and started to peck at the peg, then tried to tear out the peg with her claws, making odd sounds and working harder than ever to remove the peg. When all failed, she turned and flew off in a straight line toward the field.

It only took a few minutes for her to return, and in her bill was a blade of grass. Once she was in place, positioned to one side of the peg, she touched the reed to the peg. Bang! It was a lot louder than yesterday, or so Juddac thought. When he heard it, his first reaction was to stand up, but he caught himself in time and remained hidden. He watched the peg shoot through the air and land out in the field. The force was greater today.

Again the woodpecker made a fast check of the nest and

then started her flight. Juddac watched her start to fly in the wrong direction and he thought she was heading back to the house, when she made a sharp turn and headed for the fire. When she reached the fire, she hovered above the bright red cloth with the sun shining on it, then dropped the blade of grass almost in the center of the cloth and flew back to her nest. Fire was the method the woodpecker used to destroy the reed and keep her secret, and she thought that she had dropped the blade in the center of the flames.

Juddac couldn't move. He saw the reed but he couldn't move. When he came out of his daze he jumped up and started to run toward the fire; he fell and began to crawl on all fours. Get the reed, was the only thing on his mind. He made it to the fire and there on top of the red cloth lay the magic reed that so many had hoped to find. He was afraid to touch it, not knowing what might happen when he did. To him it looked like any one of the millions of blades in the field.

Now! Juddac said to himself, making up his mind, and he reached out to pick it up. The blade felt no different than any he had held before or the many he had placed in his mouth hundreds of times as he sat out in the fields. But he was so nervous that he dropped it and the blade fell back onto the cloth. This time Juddac hurried to pick it up again. He had a small, soft leather pouch that he used to carry his money in, so he took out the few dollars and some change and placed the reed in the bag very carefully. He sat down and put the pouch in his shirt pocket. Still in a state of shock, it felt as if he was having the best dream of his life.

Like most dreams, though, it had to end. He heard the bell of one of his cows off near the small house, so he had to hurry and turn it back to join the herd. All day long he had thought of nothing but the reed and his joy at recovering it. Many times that day he reached into his pocket and took out the small bag, looking inside to make sure it was still there.

After he returned the cows to their owners that evening

and made his way home, and after his own cow was taken care of and he had washed and had his supper, Juddac sat at his table, and with the pouch in his hand, opened it one more time now and took out the reed. Just holding it made him feel good. He lit his pipe and sat thinking, laughing to himself at how he had run for the fire when the woodpecker dropped the reed, falling and crawling on the ground.

That night when he closed his eyes, Juddac went quickly into a deep sleep, sure that his dreams would be good.

The next morning when he got out of bed he felt like the whole world was his. Even the cows today seemed to be on better behavior and took to the path leading to the field on their own. When he came to the tree near the edge of the field he looked up and saw the woodpecker pop out of her nest and fly to the field. Juddac almost felt like climbing up the tree to look in the hole and see the young birds, but changed his mind and instead took the cows to the other side of the field.

He was very careful to keep the secret to himself, and the days that followed went by without anyone having any idea that he had the reed. One day shortly after finding the reed, Juddac went to open a lock on his small storage shed and found that he had lost the key. He thought, Now would be the time to test this magic reed. So he removed the pouch from his pocket, took out the blade of grass, and was about to touch it to the lock when he remembered how the peg had flown out of the hole and into the field. Would this happen to the lock? Not sure what might take place, he made up his mind that he had to try, and standing to one side of the lock and holding the reed by one end, he made the touch.

The moment the reed touched the padlock, it opened as quietly as if he had used the key. No loud bang or great force took place, and at this Juddac was surprised.

At first he thought that maybe the reed had lost some of its power, so to make sure he closed the padlock again. When the touch was made, it opened as gently and smoothly as it had done on the first try. Juddac was sure now that the reed could open any lock or door, and whenever he was by himself the next few days, he would experiment unlocking the door to his house and other locks he had around. But always he was careful to make sure no one would see his magic.

The next week, Juddac wanted to go into town to pick up a few things at the store and to just get away from the cows for awhile, so he arranged with another herdsman to watch his cows.

While in town he met some of his friends and passed some time at the local hardware store and the feed mill, still keeping his secret to himself. It was just before noon that he was ready to start home. He came out of the market and turned the corner when he saw a large crowd in front of the bank. He walked over to the area to see what was going on and asked one of the men who was standing nearby what had happened. Andy, the man he spoke to, said that Tom Higgens, the banker, was locked in the safe and they couldn't get the door open.

When Tom had gone into the safe, the door had closed by accident, and now it was jammed. Even the chief clerk who had the combination hadn't been able to get it unlocked.

After they failed to get the safe open they had called the mechanics at the mines for help, and had even called for a locksmith from out of town. But it might be hours before he could get here, and Tom might suffocate if they didn't get the safe open soon.

As Andy was talking to Juddac, a man came out of the bank and asked the people in the crowd, now larger than before, if they had any ideas as how to open the door, or if they knew of anyone who might be able to help. But no one had any ideas other than blowing off the safe door, and this would likely mean that Tom could be killed in the blast.

About this time Juddac, now thinking of his reed and the small pouch, just reached in his pocket to make sure they were safe. He didn't want to admit that he might be able to help, because with so many people around, inside the bank and out, surely they would see him use the reed if he tried.

So as others were talking about what could be done, Juddac said that he was going on home and started down the street. As he was leaving, Jim Smith, the chief clerk, came out of the bank and made an appeal to the crowd, that if anyone had any ideas, please come forward. Juddac felt that surely they would get the door open with so much help. Besides, my reed might not work on this type of lock, he thought.

But a few hundred feet down the street, he remembered the story he had heard about a man who smothered to death locked in a room. Must of been awful, he thought to himself. Should I go back and at least make an offer to help open the safe door? After all, old Tom never done me any harm.

Now something made him turn around and go back to the bank, and down deep in his heart he knew that he must help. Returning to the place where he stood before, he heard Andy say "I guess it looks bad for Tom, because the men are working as hard as they can and still can't open the safe. The mechanics from the mines have some large tools that are big enough to open any door, but they can't budge the safe door. They say that the locksmith is on his way but the distance is a factor, and the time to travel to the bank could be an hour longer, and they're not even sure he can help."

Once again Jim Smith was outside talking to the crowd and asking for help. Jim was a good fellow and would do anything for anyone. He always talked to Juddac when he met him on the street or in church.

Juddac couldn't stand by doing nothing, so he set down his pokes, full of groceries, on the steps of the building he was standing by. He walked across the street to the bank door and told one of the men standing there that he might be able to help open the safe. The man looked at him and started to stall him, saying what they needed was a locksmith. But Jim heard the word "help," and came over to the door. Seeing Juddac, Jim said to him, "Mike, did I hear you say that you might be able to help open the door?" Jim never did call him Juddac, but always by his Christian name Michael.

"Yes," replied Juddac, "I just might be able to help."

"But how?" Jim asked.

Juddac told him that first all the people in the bank must go outside and leave him alone for a short time.

"I don't know if I can do that," Jim said, "but I'll find out if the men will go along with this request." And Jim went over to talk to the men. When he returned to the office Juddac knew what he would say from the looks he was getting from some of the men. "I'm sorry, Mike. They want to keep on working on the door because time is running out for Tom. But you can try anything you want to along with these men. You know he's been in there all too long now and they don't want to waste any time."

At this Juddac was going to leave the office. "I can't help," he told Jim, "with anyone in the bank. I just can't. I can only try to help if you and everyone else are outside."

Jim said "Wait, I'll talk to the men once more." After a few minutes he returned to Juddac, saying, "They agreed to give you a few minutes to try and do what they have failed to do in hours."

The bank was cleared, with some grumbling, and Juddac now pulled down all the blinds. The stage was set. He walked over to the safe and removed the pouch from his pocket. He then took out the magic reed and, holding his breath, he touched the reed to the door. At once the wheel turned and the door opened. Tom Higgens was on the floor, and looked like it was too late to help him. Returning the reed to his pouch, Juddac went into the safe and turned Tom over on his back. He was still breathing and soon he opened his eyes and saw Juddac bending over him. "What happened?" he asked.

Juddac told him to lie still and not move. "I'll get some help."

Juddac went over and raised the blinds and opened the door to call Jim, who had stayed close by with all the other men that had left the bank at his request. They all rushed into the bank and over to the safe to find Tom, now sitting up, dazed but alive. They pushed by Juddac like he wasn't there, an no one noticed him.

To his own surprise, Juddac walked out of the bank and across the street to where he'd left his pokes of groceries. And the crowd, not knowing what had happened, didn't pay any attention to him either. They were all moving toward the bank and wanted to see if Tom was free and alive. About now a fellow came out of the bank and shouted, "He's alive and free."

With his pokes under both arms, Juddac started down the street and was on his way home when Jim came running after him. "Mike! Mike!" he was shouting, "Wait up. I want to talk to you."

Jim, now under a full head of steam, was running and still calling to Juddac to wait. "Mike, Tom's alive and wants to talk to you. Please come back to the bank."

When they returned everyone was asking, "How did you open the safe?" But not intending to tell them, or anyone, Juddac said he had just turned the wheel and it opened.

Jim led him into the bank and on to Tom Higgens's office. Tom, still shaken by his ordeal and resting in his chair, stood up and reached out to shake Juddac's hand, thanking him over and over.

"I don't know how you did it, but I'm sure glad you did. Thanks again, and if there is anything I can do for you, please let me know."

Juddac said, "I was only too glad to help, and really, I didn't do anything but turn the wheel and the door opened. Now I guess I'd better be getting home, 'cause I've been in town too long already."

Tom wanted to drive Juddac home, but Juddac insisted on walking. "No thanks, I just feel like walking some in the fresh air." For right then Juddac's head was spinning with the excitement of his new-found magic.

Jim turned to Tom and said, "I'd like to walk Mike home if it's alright with you. I just want to walk with you, Mike, and I promise not to ask you how. I just feel like being near you and getting out of the bank for awhile." And saying goodby to Tom, they left the bank.

By now everyone outside the bank knew it was Juddac that opened the safe and freed Tom, and as he and Jim walked out of the bank Juddac was asked by everyone, "How did you do it?" Some of them were reaching out to shake his hand and still asking, "How did you free old Tom?" Now he started to worry about the reed, with all these people knowing he had opened the safe and wondering what he had done.

Even Andy, the fellow Juddac was first talking to outside the bank, came up and asked him, "Juddac, how did you get the door open?"

"I just turned the wheel and it opened, Andy." And they made their way past the crowd and down the street.

As Jim walked with him, carrying a poke full of Juddac's groceries, he turned and said, "I think from now on I'll call you Juddac, because anyone can have the name Mike, but only you can be Juddac."

On the way to Juddac's house they talked about everything but the opening of the safe door, and for the first time in his life, Juddac felt like he was someone and now had a place in life. Could this last?

It wasn't until Jim left and Juddac sat down to have a cup of coffee that he had time to think about what it meant for all those people to know of him opening the safe. This did worry him, and the more he thought about it the more he worried. But he felt too good to let it get him down. Most of the afternoon he just sat around thinking of what he might do with this magic. A man could do a lot of good with it if he tried.

The next several days were busy ones for Juddac, because now more and more people stopped by at the house to talk, and they all asked him "How?" Sunday, even though he went to early morning service, he had a hard time getting away from the same question.

The following week when he made his stops at 6:00 A.M. to pick up the cows, the women stayed near their barns after milking, just to talk to him. He knew what they wanted to know, and when asked, he would only answer, "It was easy," and move on. They all knew that he and he alone had the answer.

In the field the days seemed to pass very slowly. Juddac went by the tree a few times and always looked up, but he never looked at any of the other trees to see if he could find another woodpecker's nest.

Tom Higgens and Jim Smith stopped by to see Juddac several times and they wanted to know if they could do anything for him or if he needed any help. Juddac began to wonder if they were worried because they knew he could open the safe.

Then one day Tom stopped by at the house with a man who wanted to write a story about Juddac. He lived several miles away and worked for the paper. The man asked him many times how he managed to open the safe when all the others had failed. "I don't know. Maybe just luck," Juddac told him. "Things happened so fast that day it's hard to recall some of the events, but I just turned the wheel and the door opened."

You could see by the look on the man's face, and on Tom's, that they didn't believe him, but they left without Tom ever challenging Juddac about how he had really done it. Whatever it was, it had saved Tom's life, and that was enough for him.

A few months passed and the coming of fall meant that the cows stopped going to the field. This gave Juddac more time to himself and he could start to repair furniture. His winter months kept him busy either repairing or building furniture.

And this year more people than ever asked him to do their repairs because of the bank incident. It seemed like people from all over were coming to talk to him.

Juddac had always kept the pouch with him and never left it out of his sight. But any blade of grass will dry out and start to fall apart, and this is what happened to the reed. So Juddac now kept the pouch on a shelf more than in his pocket, because the reed was starting to break in two. This had him worried, and he spent many hours wondering how he could keep it intact.

While repairing a piece of furniture one day, he cut his finger. It was a deep cut, but not wanting to go to a doctor, he treated it himself. After supper he was sitting at the table when he thought he should check the magic reed. So he took his pouch down from the shelf and opened it and reached in to remove the blade. By now it was broken into several small pieces. As he held a few fragments in his hand, one small piece was pushed into the cut on his finger, but Juddac didn't notice. Very carefully he replaced the reed in the pouch. Then, because his cut was stinging, he put on some home-made salve and wrapped it. This pushed the piece of reed into the wound a little deeper.

A week passed by and the cut on his finger healed over, with Juddac never knowing that a small piece of the reed was embedded in it. One day he went to unlock a door, and just as his finger touched the lock, the door opened with ease. Juddac couldn't understand what had happened. He relocked the door and touched it with his finger, and it opened again.

Juddac thought back to the day he had cut his finger and realized what must have happened. And he was happy now, knowing that part of the reed would be protected if anything happened to the rest of it. This way he would always have something left of the magic reed.

It was early on a Friday morning, just after he had had breakfast and was about to get to working, when a loud knock came at the door. When he opened it to see who was there, he found a man wearing a white apron and coat and breathing hard.

The man said "Are you the man that opened the safe door?" This before Juddac had a chance to say a word. "My name is Amos, Amos Dominick. I own the meat market over in Dillstown. My son is locked in the cooler and the latch is broken off. We can't get the door open. Please come with me!"

Juddac could see he was very upset and told him to slow down.

But Amos said again, "Will you please come and open the door? I'll pay you anything, only hurry. I know Bill is in danger and I need help for him, now."

Juddac felt sorry for him, but he said to Amos, "I'm not sure I can help."

But Amos kept on pleading, "Please! I'm afraid Bill will die if we don't hurry."

So Juddac said, "I'm not sure, but I will go with you."

Amos had his small truck parked outside with the motor still running. They climbed in and Amos didn't waste any time, but started down the road, dust flying, and they hit every hole and bump. Dillstown was about ten miles away, and as Amos drove they talked about the roads and the wagons they passed on the way.

Once Amos asked Juddac how he had opened the safe when everything else failed. At this Juddac replied, "If you need the answer to that question, you had better stop the truck and leave me out."

"No! No!" Amos said, "I'm sorry I asked. Tom Higgens told me that he never asked you that question and you saved his life. I'm sorry. I won't ask it again. I only hope that you can free Bill."

Now on the road about twenty minutes, they came to the outskirts of the town and within a few minutes they pulled up to the store. On the way in they passed two of the coal mines that most of the men worked in. The company houses looked neat and clean and the people took good care of the yards. One thing about most of the miners, Juddac thought to himself, they were poor but they always kept things as clean as they could.

Several men and women were standing outside the store and a few were inside working to free Bill as they pulled up to the front door. The men were trying to pry open the door to the cooler with heavy crow bars, but it was lined with a strip of metal and they couldn't move it. The cooler was built of stone and concrete and set back into the side of an earth wall. There was no way to enter from the back or sides.

"Come with me, Juddac," Amos said.

They walked to the back part of the store and stood in front of the heavy door to the cooler. Parts of it had been broken away, but only around the edges. Some of the men, using heavy hammers, were trying to break in the wood sections, but with little effect.

"Meet Juddac," Amos told the men, and they stopped to say hello.

One of the men spoke up, saying they hadn't heard a sound from Bill for the last ten minutes. They were worried that he had fallen asleep, and it was hard to say just how bad things were. Amos turned to Juddac.

Juddac knew that he had to get the men out of the store before he made his attempt, so that no one would see him open the door. He told Amos to have the men step outside for a few minutes and leave him alone. As before, this didn't go over too well with the men, but they agreed to leave.

Amos then asked "Juddac, can I stay to help you?"

"No," he told him, "If you want me to try and open the door, do as I say or I cannot help."

So they all went outside, and when the door was closed Juddac went to work.

He walked over to the cooler and with the finger that had the magic reed he touched the heavy door. It opened like a breeze. Juddac now stepped into the cooler and found Bill huddled in a corner, cold but still alive. Juddac picked him up and carried him out of the cooler into the store and set him down in a chair. Bill, still in a state of shock and never having seen Juddac before, couldn't understand why only the two of them were in the store. He was cold and frightened and had a hard time speaking. Juddac said to him, "You'll be alright. I'll get your father."

He went to the door and called out to Amos, who was standing nearby, "He's fine and asked to see you."

Amos had only one thing on his mind, to see his son. The other men followed him into the store and, after seeing that Bill was alright went over to check out the door.

Amos, now with his arms wrapped around his son, was asking him how he felt. "Cold, but I feel fine," Bill said. "Who is that man, Dad? The one who carried me out of the cooler."

"I think he's the best friend you and I ever had," Amos replied.

Then Amos told his son that this was the man they had heard about when the safe door was opened to save Mr. Higgens, the banker. Bill got up from the chair and went over to Juddac and reached out to say thanks with his hand clasped in Juddac's.

The men were now crowding around Juddac, asking the same old question. "How? How did you get the door open?"

When Amos heard him being asked the same thing over and over he came over to Juddac. "I don't know how you did it, and I don't care. It just feels good to know you." Juddac felt good, too, and each time he looked at Bill he thanked the Lord for the reed.

Amos asked Juddac, "What do I owe you for your help? Just let me know and I will try to give you whatever you want. Saving my son is worth all I own and you can have it all."

"Just take me home, Amos, and I'm sure the thanks your

son gave me and the look in his eyes is thanks enough. In fact, that was double payment."

Well, Amos just wouldn't let Juddac leave without first taking him over to tell Amos's wife what had happened to Bill and how Juddac had surely saved their son's life. And when she heard about it, she got up from her chair and came over to Juddac, and with her hand in his, could only say, "God bless you, Juddac. God bless you."

Then they insisted on Juddac's staying for the mid-day dinner with them, and while they ate and talked and laughed, no one once asked him how he had opened the door.

Late that afternoon, when they drove Juddac back home, Amos and Bill got out too, bringing several bags of groceries out from the back of the truck.

"What's this?" Juddac asked. "You know you didn't have to do this."

"Just a few things you might be able to use," said Amos. "I just had to give you something."

Then they took his hand to thank him once more, and hoped he would come visit them again. When they drove off, Juddac felt like a little part of him had left with them.

It was late now in the afternoon and he just sat around thinking of the day and how it all started. He thought about the reed and how much good it had done for others and what it had done for him. It had given him a feeling of belonging, for he had been able to truly help these people.

A day passed and once again the folks in town heard about him getting the Campbell boy out of the meat cooler and this meant everyone started stopping by to say hello. Juddac didn't mind, though, because it made him feel good.

Tom Higgens stopped by and found Juddac in the work shed in back of the house fixing a hand tool he used for his woodworking. Tom said, "I heard about the Dominick boy and just about everyone for miles around has also. You are well known, Juddac, and in town everyone is talking about you. I, for one, only hope you can keep on doing good for anyone that might need your help.

"And Juddac," Tom went on, "I came here today because I want to talk to you about something else that could be important to me and you."

"Well," said Juddac to Tom, "let's go into the house and sit down to that cup of coffee you favor, and you can tell me what's on your mind."

When they were seated at the table, Tom leaned forward and spoke. "Juddac, I would like you to come and work for me. The job would give you a better way of living, and it would help me too."

At this Juddac said, "Tom, you know I know nothing about banking, and it would be all wrong for me to even think of it."

So Tom said "I know nothing about mixing feeds and taking care of animals, and you do. I want you to work the feed mill for me, Juddac, not the bank. You know I own the mill, and with your experience with farm animals you would be great at blending the feeds and mixes. You'll be well paid and you are entitled to it," Tom said. "I know this better than anyone. I've thought about this for several weeks, so please say yes because it can make us both feel good. And Juddac," he went on, "you know the home I own near the mill. Well, I would like you to move into it rent-free for as long as you want it. It's a nice place and has a plot for a garden or whatever you want to use it for."

As Juddac said yes to Tom, he thought back over all that had happened to him since he first recovered the magic reed. It seemed like the woodpecker's blade of grass had not only opened real doors and locks for him, but now was even opening the door to a better way of life. For the first time in his life he was going to have a good job with regular wages. Then Juddac remembered how a man had once told him that a person should not worry about what his place in life might be, for it was already provided for according to God's plan. Maybe his time had come, and Juddac wondered if he would be worthy.

The next few days Juddac was busy. He sold his cow and made arrangements for the others to be watched by another herdsman. He sold or gave away what little he had in the way of furnishings, since the house near the mill was already fixed up with everything he would need. But he kept his woodworking tools and an old family chest and, of course, the pouch with his magic reed.

The night before he was to start his new job at the mill, it was as bad as the time he first discovered the woodpecker's secret. Juddac tossed and turned, too excited to get to sleep and a little worried about whether the men working at the mill would accept him in his new job. But when he reached the mill in the early morning, he found all the men waiting there to greet him, and Tom Higgens with them.

Tom took the honor of showing Juddac to the office, and there on a desk was a sign that read in bold letters, JUDDAC. Then he introduced Juddac to the others and to Betty, who handled the office phones and paperwork. Tom asked Stush, one of the mill hands, to show Juddac the rest of the mill while he got back to the bank.

As they walked from room to room and floor to floor, Juddac remembered the times past when he had come to the mill for feed. Of course now he would be supplying rather than buying. This was a big place, with lots to do if you wanted to keep things moving. Most of the local farm people came to the mill for feed and grain, and a lot of miners, too, kept a cow and raised chickens for milk and eggs to help feed their families.

So Juddac spent the day finding his way around and talking with the other workers. Once he was walking by one of the back doors and his finger accidentally touched the lock just as Stush came by.

"Someone must have left this door open," Stush told Juddac, "because they always keep it locked."

Juddac saw that he was going to have to be careful, and several times he caught himself just in time.

When it came time to close the mill for the day, Jim Smith from the bank came into the office and handed the keys to Juddac.

"Tom's orders. You will open and close the mill from now on. In fact, you're to be in charge."

Juddac turned and saw the other men standing by, smiling.

"Thanks," he said, "I guess I'll see you all in the morning."

In the weeks that followed Juddac was careful not to touch any locks in the mill unless he was alone. In the mornings, if men were waiting for him before he arrived, he always got the key out before he touched the door, sometimes handing the key to one of the men and telling him to open up.

Business at the mill, which had always been good, started picking up even more because of Juddac, partly because people who had heard stories about him wanted to see and meet him in person, but partly too because of Juddac's special blends of feed. Farmers and miners who used to come to his cottage to buy feed from Juddac when he was tending cows now started coming to the mill. Everyone was pleased with the new arrangements.

When Juddac had time off from the mill, he sometimes walked back out to the field and wooded section that had brought him to his good fortune. The old tree where the woodpecker's nest had been was now toppled, blown down by the wind or just fallen with age. He wondered if the tree would ever take care of another bird's nest.

The stories about Juddac had been growing so that by now it seemed he had performed some miracle in just about every town around and had saved dozens of people. None of these stories were true, but when one got started everyone added to it, and by the time it got around to Juddac's ears, he learned that he had accomplished things even his magic reed could never do.

But finally there did come a day when Juddac was called to use his special power again.

About 1:00 P.M. on a Tuesday, a man came rushing into the mill and said he was looking for Juddac. When he got to the office, Betty thought something must be wrong or someone injured because the man was worked up and out of breath when he said to her, "I must talk to Juddac. Tom Higgens sent me over here from the bank." Betty told him to sit down and that she would find Juddac.

She went to the blending room and called Juddac. She told him that a man had been sent over by Tom, and as they returned to the office the man was already standing and began talking fast. "Juddac, my name is Albert Scott and I'm the outside foreman at number 3, Red Mill Mines. We have a problem at the mines and Mr. Higgens said it would be alright with him for you to come over to the mines and help if you could, or if you wanted to. Please, will you come with me to the mines? I have my car outside and I'll tell you what happened on the way over, but we must hurry. It's been a while now since the cage got stuck.

"What?" Juddac asked him. "You said the elevator is stuck? I know nothing about machinery, let alone mine equipment."

But Albert said, "Maybe there's something you can do and I'm sure the men trapped will feel better knowing you are there. Please will you come?"

Juddac now said, "I'll go with you and if there is anything I can do to help I will, but I want to tell you again that I know nothing about mine machinery.

"You'll do just fine," Albert said as they got into his car. "I feel better already just knowing you will be there and I'm sure the men in the cage will feel the same."

On the way Albert continued, "I want to tell you what happened. You know the cage that the men are raised with and lowered into the mines. Well today it was about halfway up the shaft with ten men on, when it froze up. We've been fighting it for hours and can't budge it. It's stuck about a hundred feet below the ground. I think the main up-haul pinion gears are locked."

Juddac looked at him doubtfully and said, "What?" So Albert told him how that's a machine that forms part of the elevator, to lower or raise the cage.

"Better yet, we'll be there shortly and then I can show you what I mean.

"You know, around our town everyone has heard about how you saved over a hundred people. They say you can unlock any door or vault. Is this true?"

At this Juddac said, "You know how stories get started. I'll tell you again, with what I know about mine machinery it might be better for you to turn around and take me back to the mill."

"Hey, I'm sorry if it sounded like I was making fun. Truly, most of the men stranded in the cage asked to have you come and try to free them. Some of their families even came and requested that you be asked to help."

As Al pulled into the mine yard, men were running in and out of the hoist house, the building that housed the machinery used to raise and lower the cage. Everyone was too busy to notice them when they stopped at the rear of the hoist room.

"Come with me," Al told Juddac, and they made their way into the building through the back door and climbed two flights of stairs overlooking the machinery that serviced the cage. Puffing a little, Albert pointed to the shaft and gears that were frozen up and said to Juddac, "I think the trouble is in there."

Looking down at the machinery, Juddac thought, My God, what can I do? I know nothing about this type of machinery.

As they watched, the men were now working around the drum and cable that was attached to the cage. They were also checking the gears and trying to free the shaft on the floor below them. One of the men working below called to Al, "We are going down to the next level to see if we can move the pinion gear on the lower shaft."

"OK," Al said, "I'll be right down."

Then Al showed Juddac the main gears and shaft that he felt was causing the problem. He told him that in order for the drum to turn, to wind up the cable, they must first free the main pinion gear.

Juddac could see several of the men below talking together and glancing up at where he and Al were, but they never once made any remarks. Juddac now was thinking to himself, this is not a lock or a safe. This is something that I've never tried the reed on. And he had doubts that he could help or even begin to try.

But as Al and Juddac were checking the machinery, he moved his hand toward the shaft and his finger touched it. At once the machinery jerked, and everyone below started shouting, warning people to clear away from the machinery.

Al told Juddac, "Come on, get out of here. This thing might start to move. I'm going down below for a few minutes to see what happened, and you stay over here on the walkway till I get back. You don't want to be close in, just in case it starts to move."

Juddac had felt the shaft jerk when he touched it, but as his hand moved free of the shaft it had stopped. Now he felt that his reed just might work.

Al went down below and was talking to the men, trying to see what had made the machine move. They were standing clear of the gears and the shaft and Juddac could see that the way the light was shining below it made it hard for them to see him on the second floor. Thinking he would take advantage of this, he moved from the walkway over to the shaft that Al had pointed out to him. This was the one he had touched when the machine jerked a few minutes ago.

Now Juddac reached out and again touched the shaft, and the shaft and gears made another jerk that moved the cable.

The men below all started to shout, "It moved! It moved!" And Juddac, a little shaken himself and surprised at what had happened, stepped back when the shaft turned.

Al was shouting as loud as he could for Juddac to stand clear. But Juddac moved forward again and placed his hand over the grease-covered shaft. As he made the touch, the shaft started to turn and the cable started winding around the drum. The men below were still shouting for him to stand clear of the machinery, but in the excitement no one noticed what he was doing. At that moment the men didn't care why or how it was happening. They just kept shouting, "It's moving! It's moving!" And Juddac kept his hand on the shaft.

Now the drum was turning faster and the cable was winding and snapping into place as it brought the cage to the surface. They could hear the trapped men in the cage below yelling with joy that it was moving, and everyone now was waiting for the bell to ring that meant the cage was at the top of the mine shaft.

Juddac heard the elevator operator shout in a loud voice, "It's almost to the top." And when the cable jerked and the bell rang out, Juddac let go of the shaft. The drum stopped turning and everything stood still the moment he took his hand off the shaft.

Then the door to the cage opened and out sprang the men, all wanting to get free at the same time. Two of them to the rear of the cage just stood in a daze, but then jumped quickly from the cage. The men inside had been quiet and frightened during the long wait, and now free, they let out all their feelings, shouting to each other and to the men who had been trying to free them.

Some were hugging each other, some were laughing, others had tears in their eyes. One man said that when the cage reached the top, and the bell sounded, it was like hearing the bells of St. Peter's Cathedral. They all knew that it was over, but the time spent in the limbo, trapped in the cage, had given each of them a new outlook on life.

After the cage stopped and all the men were out, Al managed to push through the crowd and make his way to the stairs, rushing to see if Juddac was alright.

"I'm fine," said Juddac. "What happened?"

"You did it! You did it, Juddac!" Al told him.

"I didn't do a thing, Al," Juddac answered, but Al never heard the remark.

"You made it move, you moved the machinery. I don't know how, but you did. What did you do?"

"Nothing, I told you. I didn't do a thing. It must have been the men below that started the machinery," Juddac insisted.

Now Al reached to shake Juddac's hand, and when he let go he had a fist full of grease. It was the old grease from the shaft, and Juddac knew that Al was now sure he had put his hand on the shaft and that he was near the machinery when the cable started moving.

Al reached into his back pocket, took out a rag, and handed it to Juddac. "Here, you'd better wipe off your hand."

The men were shouting and calling for Juddac, and as Al and Juddac reached the bottom of the stairs they rushed over to him, all trying to take his hand at once. They all felt that he had saved them, and no one could change their minds. Not even Juddac.

Everyone started to move to the outside of the building and as the men stepped out you could hear the happy greetings from families waiting to see their fathers, brothers, and husbands. When each one stepped out there were loud cheers and clapping.

Then Al and Juddac came through the door, and everyone, the men and their families, started to holler and cheer. Even the chief superintendent of the mines was there waiting to greet Juddac and thank him. Some of the men approached and asked "How did you free up the machinery?" But luckily for Juddac everyone was talking at the same time so he didn't really have to give an answer. A few times Al broke in and changed the subject.

The superintendent told Al, "Take Juddac over to my office and I'll be right in. I would like to talk to him for a few minutes." So with Juddac by the arm, Al led him to the super's office. As they made their way through the crowd people were reaching out just to say hello and touch his hand. It was a hero's welcome, and Juddac could tell they meant it.

When they finally reached the office, Al said to Juddac, "I'll get the coffee on and we can have a cup."

"Sounds good to me," Juddac replied, and went into the washroom.

The super had not arrived yet when Al set a cup of coffee on the desk for Juddac. He looked him square in the eyes and asked, "How did you manage to unlock the gears? I know it had to be you, Juddac, because no one was even near the machinery." Then he said to Juddac, in still a lower voice, being careful that no one would overhear him, "Juddac, the power for the machinery was never even turned on. I doubt if it has been yet. There's no other way it could have moved unless it was something you did."

Juddac was at a loss for words, and after a short sip of coffee, said only that he had to think this out.

"Only you and I know about the power," Al went on. "As for the grease on your hand, it had to be something you did to the machine that started the hoist. The others may think that just by being there you brought good luck, and I won't try to force you to tell me what you did, but I know now that you really do have some kind of power more incredible than anything I've ever seen."

Just about the time Al finished talking, the superintendent walked into the office and Juddac was introduced to some of the foremen from around the mine who wanted to meet him.

Juddac was relieved that Al could not question him more just then, because he didn't know what answer he could give.

Once again, Juddac was asked to stay around. He and Al were both invited to dinner at the superintendent's house, and everyone stayed late talking and laughing. It seemed that people just wanted to be near Juddac somehow, and again he enjoyed the feeling of belonging and having a place in life.

It was not until Juddac got home later that night that he had a chance to sit down and think about what Al had said.

No one else had ever had any proof or clue as to how Juddac was able to help. He had always been so careful not to let anyone around when he used the magic of the woodpecker's blade. But the grease on his hand had started Al thinking, and the fact that the power had not been on when the cage moved was too much evidence for Juddac to deny.

Could he trust Al not to tell the others? And when the others did find out, what would happen? The questions and stories and fussing over him would only get worse. He wouldn't feel like he belonged anymore, he would feel like a sideshow.

Juddac was not the kind of man who could live comfortably with all that attention, and he decided that night that something had to be done.

First, though, he thought to himself, he had better check on his magic reed, for who knew how long the little sliver in his finger would keep its power? He went to the chest where he kept the pouch. When he opened the small bag and placed its contents carefully on the table, he saw that the reed had now broken into many small pieces. Worried that it soon might turn to dust and be lost, he thought about planting another piece of the reed in one of his other fingers, since he had not been able to think of any other plan to save it.

He lit a candle on the table and was holding his knife in the flame to ready it for making a cut, when he knocked the candle, just a little, but enough to cause a small trickle of wax to run down onto the table where the fragments of grass were spread. Juddac moved quickly to remove the wax with his knife, and when he scraped it up he discovered that several small splinters of the reed were now embedded in the hardening wax.

"This is the answer!" he cried out, and straight away he tested the wax on his door. As soon as he made the touch, the door unlocked smoothly and quietly, just as it did when he used his finger.

Now sure that the reed was preserved and secure, Juddac felt that he should do something for himself. Maybe this was selfish, he thought, but after all I've done for the others I should think of myself at least a little. With the pouch in his hand he sat back enjoying the thrill of his new life.

He thought how easy it could all collapse, if his secret became known, and he knew that sooner or later he would have to trust someone with the knowledge. But who?

The desire for wealth and fame made him feel foolish. This could drag a man down to ruin and destruction because "the love of money is the root of all evil." Some men that gained both wealth and the passion for it have come to grief and great pain afterwards. They let themselves be captured by this foolishness and slavery.

However well-off and prosperous his new power made him, he had to remember that it wasn't obtained by his hand alone. This reminder was renewed daily since his discovery, as he thanked the Lord.

Juddac felt that he had to look for a new life somewhere else and that he would have to put something together. This was not a sudden interest of his. Besides, he could do a lot of good for others in any area, he thought.

He returned the pouch to its place in the chest and went into the bedroom. Settling himself in bed, he felt an odd fluttering of his heart as he turned to fall asleep and dream of this new life.

The next morning, when all of the business was taken care of at the mill and things had slowed down before noon,

Juddac had some time to think on this new life idea. He sat down and leaned back in his chair and made up his mind to be a "now" person. Live in the now, he told himself. Open your eyes and take a good look around. There are so many things you can do with yourself, but whatever you do, don't hang onto a defeating attitude. Just let go of regrets and worries, and move forward. Leave all the negative attitudes behind.

Loneliness is a problem, he thought. The widespread stories of him meant someone always wanted to write or tell about him, and most of his friends in town had their own version to tell, but even with all the attention he received, loneliness was still a part of his daily life—a part of keeping his secret. Still, he wasn't the only one who felt alone. He knew more people with the problem of loneliness than of too much affection.

As he relaxed in the chair he was drifting off into more deep thinking, when Stush came into the office and sat down. Stush, a man of good humor, had risen above the labor of the mill and now talked deals with the bankers. He always had a deal cooking and today's tale would be no funnier than last week's. But Juddac thought a visit with Stush would take his mind off the two newspaper reporters wanting an interview, and the laughs and relaxation, he felt, would do him some good. It was just about lunch time, so Juddac looked up at the big clock and said, "Let's go to lunch."

Several days passed and things were back to normal at the mill. That is, almost. Juddac had a note from Betty that read, "Joshua would like you to go over to his farm. He said that it is very important, and hoped you could make it today." This will be just a short trip over to Nicktown, he thought, as he put the note in his pocket.

The men were busy taking care of customers and when Betty got back in the office, he told her that he was going over to the bank and then out to Joshua's farm.

"Don't know what time I'll be back," Juddac said.

"We'll take care of things and lock up if you're not back till late," Betty told him.

Juddac walked into the bank, feeling more uneasy than anytime since he first unlocked the safe. He didn't know why, but the feeling was there. He found himself reliving that day's events, and it wasn't until Tom called his name that he came back to reality and walked over to the office.

Tom said, "I have been meaning to come over to the mill. Glad you made it over. Have a chair. I know things have kept you on your toes since the mine rescue, and I can feel for you, Juddac—so if you need help, let me know."

"I had a letter from my sister last week and she asked me to visit with her," Juddac said. "There's no hurry, so I wrote and told her that I would make the trip, but first I had to take care of a few details here."

"Juddac, you decide whatever you want to do," Tom told him.

"Before I make the trip we should have a talk, but maybe it would be a good idea for us to talk someplace other than the office."

"I understand," Tom nodded.

"Maybe we can walk out in the wooded and field area later on this week. It might save a lot of words."

"It will give us privacy, too," Tom added.

The strictest privacy is what would be needed for this talk, because Juddac had made up his mind to trust Tom with the secret of the reed. He felt that if anyone could be trusted with it, Tom was the person. Of course he didn't want to say anything today. This would have to wait until they were alone, and then he could tell him how he had recovered the reed. If I showed Tom the wooded area near the field and explained how I found the woodpecker's nest, this might help to get it across, he thought. Juddac was not sure yet just how he would tell Tom, but he knew that a trust had to be made, just in case anything happened to him.

Juddac left the bank and was going to head on over to Nicktown to see what Joshua need him for today. While he was still in town, though, he stopped in for a bite to eat before making the short trip to the farm. Wasn't really hungry, but it tasted good. Mae's lunches were always good.

Nicktown looked down across sloping cornfields, two miles north. The village consisted of ten houses and a small general store, plus a scattering of barns, pigpens, and chicken houses. Joshua's farm was just on the outskirts of town.

On a summer afternoon the whole place dozed under a silence broken only by the occasional cluck of a hen or the clack of a closing door. This was the center of the universe, Juddac felt. He thought that this place could be named Innocence, USA—or Challenge, because why a town was built there in the first place is a mystery. The village sat a half mile back from the only hard road in the area. To get in from the highway, you had to wind through thick stands of woods along a deep-rutted dirt road that could swallow a truck all the way to the axles.

It was a hot afternoon as Juddac moved through the majestic depths of silence, a silence so immense he felt he could hear the oats growing. But under this silencing of all human noise, there was an orchestra of natural music playing notes no town folk would ever hear. As he moved across the yard toward the house he heard a cackle from the hen house that meant Joshua had gained an egg. The creak of a porch swing told of a momentary breeze blowing across the yard. He tiptoed along the walkway to the house so as not to surprise Josh, asleep on the porch, padded onto the porch and into the shade, and flopped into a chair near a window, where he could hear the pendulum clock ticking the hours away.

Juddac had just started to enjoy the shade when Joshua lifted his hat and said, "Hi. Didn't hear you come up on the porch. I must of dozed." Now on his feet he reached out his hand to Juddac. "Just sit and relax a while and I'll get something cool to drink."

"Sounds good to me. That's the best offer I've had all day, Josh."

Diane, or Annie, as Josh called his wife, came out with a tray of glasses and a pitcher of lemonade. They were enjoying the shade and cool drink when Joshua mentioned a problem with one of the heifers. Juddac didn't really think there was a problem, but he knew Josh wanted to talk. Annie sensed this and excused herself, saying that she had some work to do.

As she departed Juddac thought to himself how farmers, like miners, and especially the women, worked hard and long. It was astonishing that they had any energy left, after a day's work, to comfort the family. Their lives were hard, endless labor. They had no eletricity, plumbing, radios, washing machines, or refrigerators, yet performed wonders.

For dishwashing, baths, drinking, and laundry, they hauled buckets of water from a well or spring. It was considered a luxury to have a well with a pump nearby. To heat their water they chopped kindling and used coal to fire their stoves. They boiled laundry in copper boilers, scrubbed it by hand on a knuckle-buster called a washboard, and wrung it out by hand. Heavy metal weights, heated on the stove top, were used for ironing.

They scrubbed floors on hands and knees, killed and plucked their own chickens, grew and canned their own vegetables, rose before daylight to start the stove for breakfast. They even found time to tend the flowers that grew around the house. By the end of every day the women had toiled like slaves. It was strange that even with all their hardship, you could hear them singing a hymn as they worked.

We had finished the refreshment when Annie made her appearance again and asked if we wanted anything. "No thanks. We better get going." She was a delicate woman, with blonde hair and a way of turning her head suddenly this way and that which reminded me of an alert bird. She was a notoriously fussy housekeeper, constantly battling the dust.

Juddac told Josh he was going to make a quick trip to the outhouse and then he would be ready to go check out the heifer. Arriving at a two-hole privy he found the standard bathroom paper, a mail-order catalogue—a luxury too rich to use by most folks around.

When he met Joshua at the barn, Josh told Juddac that the cows were alright. "The reason I wanted you to come out today was to talk. You and I might have the same interest."

"I figured something was up when I came to the house today and you were on the porch early this afternoon," replied Juddac.

"I don't know how to begin, so maybe you can help me out as I tell you what's on my mind."

"Be glad to if I can," Juddac said.

Joshua began, "I wanted to go to your house or to the mill a thousand times in the past six months. Never could bring myself to talk to you, even when I seen you at the mill or in town, and I wanted to more than I can say. It all started after the news of you freeing Tom, and the day you went over to Dillstown.

"Then it was you who saved the men at the mines, and that made me think for sure you found what I have been searching for for a long time. I have searched for years to find the mysterious power that could do things beyond belief."

At this, Juddac could only think of one power—the magic reed.

Joshua continued, "When I was a boy, my grandfather told the tale of a magic blade of grass."

Now Juddac was sure Joshua was looking for the reed, but before he had a chance to say a word, Joshua went on with his story.

"As a boy, it didn't mean a whole lot the first time I heard the tale. But when it was told time and time again, I started to believe it more."

At this point Juddac was almost ready to speak out and say he knew nothing of the woodpecker and its reed, but he remained quiet.

Now Joshua, feeling a little more at ease, relaxed and said, "Let's walk over to the meadow and I can show you the place where it really became a dream come true for me."

Juddac once again felt like he should turn and say good-by, but he went with Joshua towards the field.

As they walked Joshua said, "You had to search for it where the crabgrass grew and choked out the narrow leaves of good meadow grass. This is where you had to search for it, and the remarkable power could be yours."

He went on to say, "You must pull up or cut this grass and toss it into a stream where the water flowed swiftly. When the grass hit the water it would float downstream with the current, but then if one blade turned and floated upstream, you must recover it, because it possessed the strange powers."

Juddac now looked at him and asked, "What kind of power?"

"It was told," Joshua said, "that it would make you strong, intellectual, wise, and above all would give you a form of magical power."

They were walking towards the north meadow now and Joshua told him, "As a kid, all of these fields and meadows were my playgrounds and I never passed a stream or brook without throwing in several handfuls of grass. Then I'd stand by to watch for the one that might float upstream. I would say that up until the time Annie and I got married, this ritual was repeated several thousand times. It became an obsession with me once, but kids have a way of leaving go, you know what I mean?

"After years of trying, when you're full grown you kind of put an idea away. I did, until one day I was returning from the north pasture and stopped here on this footbridge. I leaned on the railing to rest a few minutes, looking down into the water that flows fast here, watching the bits and pieces of wood float past, and then I seen what I believed was the object of this legend and a life's search."

Juddac, now more relieved because this tale had nothing to do with his magic reed, began to hope for Joshua.

Joshua told how, as he looked at the water, to his disbelief a blade of grass moved out from under where he was standing and moved swiftly upstream against the current. It appeared and moved as if it were powered by some mysterious force.

"I seen it and then hesitated a second or two before running down to the stream, trying to keep my eyes on the blade and follow it to make sure it would not be lost. As I reached the edge of the water, it seemed to disappear around that small bend," pointing it out to Juddac.

Joshua's voice dropped a few tones and Juddac knew how he felt. Juddac remembered the day at the edge of the woods and how he first thought he had the reed and then all was lost.

Joshua broke the silence in a low voice. "Until that day I had resolved to give up the searching I had done as a boy, but when this happened, I think it made me look harder than before and spend several hours each week trying to find it. Maybe I was never meant to have it, and if this is so, let it be.

"I'll never let it take any time away from Annie and the family or from my daily duties, because this could ruin a man's life. Nothing is worth that, not even wealth or power."

"I more than anyone can share that feeling with you," Juddac told him.

They walked over to the bank beside the stream and sat down. Juddac said out loud, not meaning to, "At the moment of my defeat, I was laying plans for my next try."

"What did you say, Juddac?"

"I guess I must of been thinking out loud," he replied.

Juddac turned to Joshua and said, "You have a headstart on most, because of what happened that day. Besides, you also have a fine wife and family and a good farm with a lot of future."

"I know this, and feel I just should give up the idea of finding it. You are the first to know of my search," Joshua said, "and the only reason I'm telling you is because you are my friend and I know I can trust you, and because we've been friends long before you were outstanding and well-known."

Juddac looked him in the eye and said, "Thank you for making me worthy."

Joshua never asked Juddac about his power, today or anytime since they knew he had something that no one else had. He did say to Juddac, "I only feel bad not knowing if that blade of grass really has any strength or what it does possess. I guess I'll keep up the search, at least for awhile."

Getting up, both men walked back to the footbridge and stood there for a few minutes just looking down at the water. It still had some bits and pieces of wood floating by.

They left the stream and started the walk back towards the house, a quarter of a mile away. Didn't say much until they reached a special place.

As they walked along Juddac was in deep thought about what he wanted to do about his secret. He felt as if he wanted to entrust it now with Joshua, because they had the same desires in life. But if he told him about his own blade it might drive him on to the point that he would forget about everything, including his family. This could ruin their lives. Then he thought about Joshua and the years he had spent looking for this power and how he was as good and fair as any man. It didn't seem to pull him down. After all, he has been searching longer than I, Juddac thought. If I told him it just might satisfy him and ease his mind.

They were a few hundred feet from the house now and the special place was a small shrine Joshua and his father built many years ago. It was well taken care of and the family always stopped there going to and from the fields to say a prayer.

As they stood there in silence, something seemed to move

inside of Juddac and he turned to Joshua and said, "There is something I feel you should know, and I want to entrust my secret with you for safekeeping."

So Juddac told his story. And Joshua, now wide eyed, listened with enthusiasm, asking Juddac to repeat certain parts to make sure he knew every detail.

When Juddac finished his final word he said to Joshua, "I have told you, because I too find you worthy of my trust." Juddac never told Joshua that he had first had Tom in mind for his secret, and Tom himself did not know. Hand in hand, Juddac and Joshua sealed their words for friendship's sake.

Annie was out on the porch when they got back to the house. She wanted Juddac to stay for supper, and he thanked her but told her he had to get back to town. He told Joshua that he planned to go away for a while and that he would keep in touch with him.

"I'll see you before I go because you're sure to be in town for some feed in a few days."

Juddac said his farewell and departed.

Diane noticed a gleam in Joshua's eyes but really didn't know what it was about. He only told her at supper that today was a day he would remember as long as he lived. She did see that Joshua had the appearance of a different man, though it might be a while before she would find out why.

The next few weeks were busy ones for Juddac. He had his talk with Tom and told him why he wanted to go away, but Tom had known a long time ago. Juddac told him that he would be in touch with him and maybe he would return to the place he would always call home.

There was a strong bond of quiet friendship between the two men, and Juddac knew he would always be welcome.

Before Juddac left, Joshua came by the mill to say goodby. They shook hands and nodded to each other with a knowing smile.

48

It now has been five years since Juddac moved away.

Joshua heard from him a year ago.

Tom had a letter from him about the same time.

Both men wait and look for another letter or card, hoping it might come today.